Invasion of the Mind Swappers from Asteroid 6!

Tales from the House of Bunnicula Books by James Howe:
It Came from Beneath the Bed!
Invasion of the Mind Swappers from Asteroid 6!

Other Bunnicula Books by James Howe:

Bunnicula (with Deborah Howe)
Howliday Inn
The Celery Stalks at Midnight
Nighty-Nightmare
Return to Howliday Inn
Bunnicula Strikes Again!

James Howe is the author of the award-winning bestseller, *Bunnicula*, and its sequels, as well as many other popular books for young readers, including *The Misfits* and the Pinky and Rex series for younger readers. He lives in Hastings-on-Hudson, New York.

TALES FROM THE HOUSE OF BUNNICULA

Invasion of the Mind Swappers from Asteroid 6!

JAMES HOWE
ILLUSTRATED BY BRETT HELQUIST

SCHOLASTIC INC.
New York Toronto London Auckland Sydney
Mexico City New Delhi Hong Kong Buenos Aires

ISBN 0-439-52481-4

Text copyright © 2002 by James Howe.
Illustrations copyright © 2002 by Brett Helquist. All rights reserved.
Published by Scholastic Inc., 557 Broadway, New York, NY 10012 by arrangement
with Atheneum Books for Young Readers, a Simon & Schuster Children's Publishing
Division. SCHOLASTIC and associated logos are trademarks and/or registered
trademarks of Scholastic Inc.

12 11 10 9 8 7 6 5 4 3 2 1   3 4 5 6 7 8/0

Printed in the U.S.A.   40

First Scholastic printing, March 2003

Book design by Ann Bobco

The text of this book is set in Berkeley.

The illustrations are rendered in acrylics and oils.

To Marvia Boettcher,
who has the best laugh west of the Mississippi
—J. H.

For Mary Jane
—B. H.

Dear Howie Monroe:

I am in receipt of the manu-
script of your book, *It Came from
Beneath the Bed!* I found the tale
gripping and would be honored if
you would allow me to publish it.
However, I believe it would work
best as part of a series. Please
send me another book as soon as
possible. When I have received
it, I will send you a contract
and a check.

Sincerely yours,
The Editor

HOWIE'S WRITING JOURNAL

Wow! Uncle Harold sent my first book, <u>It Came from Beneath the Bed!</u>, to his editor, and he's going to publish it! Now I'm not just a writer, I'm an <u>author</u>!!!!

The only problem is I have to write another book.

Writing one book was fun. But having to write another one sounds like work!

What if I used up all my ideas on the first book? What if I never have another idea again? Ever?!

Wait a minute, I can't give up before I even start. Let's see. The first book was called It Came from Beneath the Bed!, so maybe I can call the second one It Came from Behind the Refrigerator!

Or It Came from Inside the Garbage Can!

Or It Came from Around the Corner of the Woodshed When the Moon Was Full and the Zombies Howled!

Good one. Or . . .

I'm getting a headache. It came from too much thinking!

Who am I kidding? I'm not an author, I'm just a lovable, adorable, smart, and talented wirehaired dachshund puppy who got lucky.

What if I <u>were</u> an author, though? I mean, like a <u>person</u> author? What would it be like to be someone other than me?

What if I could be turned into someone else?

But why? Why would somebody want to turn me into anything other than the lovable, adorable, smart, and talented wirehaired dachshund puppy that I am?

Uncle Harold, who has written a whole bunch of books, says the best way to make a story happen is by asking lots of questions.

So, okay, what if there was somebody who wanted to turn cute little puppies and other people into something else?

And what if whoever it was came from someplace really far away? Like Cleveland. Or Mars.

That's it! I know what my next book will be!

Who says writing is hard?

Invasion of the Mind Swappers from Asteroid 6!

By Howie Monroe

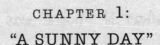

CHAPTER 1:
"A SUNNY DAY"

It was a sunny day in the peaceful little village of Centerville. Howie, a lovable, adorable, smart, and talented wirehaired dachshund puppy (who was also humble), was on his way to his friend Delilah's house.

It sure is a sunny day, the observant puppy thought. *On a day like this, nothing can go wrong.*

Just then, he heard a strange sound. Was it

thunder? Impossible! Howie shrugged and continued on his way until he spotted Delilah basking on her back on the sidewalk in front of her house. "Delilah!" he yipped.

"Howie!" Delilah yipped back.

It was wonderful how easily they communicated.

"I was hoping you would come over today," Delilah said, putting her paws on the ground instead of up in the air, where they'd been just moments before. "Do you want to play Rip-the-Rag? Or how about Knock-Each-Other-Down?"

How could Howie decide? They were *both* his favorite games! "You choose," he told Delilah.

Delilah sighed. "Oh, Howie," she said, "you are such a gentleman."

Howie had to agree.

Delilah tossed her blonde ears and cocked her head to one side. She thought and thought. Finally, she said, "Thinking is hard work."

Howie nodded. Delilah was beautiful, but not very bright. "Take your time," he told her.

Delilah thought some more and finally said, "I think we should play—"

But her sentence was cut off by the strange sound Howie had heard on his way over. "Thunder?" he wondered aloud.

"I don't know how to play that one," said Delilah. "Will you teach me?"

"No," Howie said. "I was talking about that strange sound. Did you hear it?"

"Oh, that," said Delilah. "It's probably just a lawn mower."

Howie shook his head. "It's not like any lawn mower I ever heard. I think we should go investigate."

"All right," said Delilah. "But then can we play Rip-the-Rag?"

"Sure," Howie told her as they set off in the direction of the strange sound.

Little did he know that they might never play Rip-the-Rag—or any of their favorite games—again!!!!

Howie's Writing Journal

I showed my first chapter to Uncle Harold.

I said, "So what do you think, Uncle Harold? Huh, huh, huh?"

He said, "I think you're using too many adjectives about a certain character just the way you did in your first book, but I like the way you ended the chapter. The cliff-hanger is excellent."

I'm glad he liked my cliff-hanger, but I'm

beginning to suspect that Uncle Harold has a hang-up about adjectives.

Then he asked me if the strange sound was a can opener. I figure he asked that because he was hungry. Of course, Uncle Harold is always hungry. I am too. We're dogs. But it's not a can opener.

Oh, even though Uncle Harold didn't say anything about it, I decided I'd better change Delilah's character. My real friend Delilah (who is beautiful and smart, too) got angry with me after I wrote my first book because of the way I'd made her character kind of stupid. I promised I'd make her smarter in this book.

So I guess I should go back and rewrite the last chapter. But I don't want to. I'm lazy.

Uncle Harold says this is not a good trait in a writer.

I reminded him I'm an <u>author</u> now. He said I need to watch out for arrogance. I told him if I saw any coming at me, I'd duck.

He didn't laugh. I think his hang-up about adjectives is making him lose his sense of humor.

"That was fun, pretending to be dumb," said Delilah as she jogged alongside Howie. "But you know that I'm really smart, don't you?"

"Of course," said Howie.

Delilah said, "Do you know what twelve to the fourth power divided by seventeen is? I do. Do you know who the sixth president of the United States was? I do. Can you spell antidisestablishmentarianism? I can."

"Watch out for arrogance," Howie said.

Delilah ducked.

Soon they came to an open field.

"Listen," said Howie, whose keen ears had picked up the strange sound again.

Delilah squinted. "I hear it, too," she said. "It sounds larger than a lawn mower. But it is definitely the sound of something moving. I would say that whatever it is, is moving a fraction less than the speed of sound itself. Of course, the speed of sound is not a constant. It varies depending on the medium in which it travels. If we assume that the sound we are hearing is traveling in the medium of air, then we must take into account such factors as air pressure, the temperature, and, obviously, the purity of the air itself, which is no small matter given the effect of pollution these days. Now, at sea level—"

"You are *too* smart," Howie said. "I'm going to have to revise you."

Delilah had no answer to this.

Just then, a weird voice said, "Cease, earthlings!"

Howie and Delilah looked around. There was no one in sight. They took a few more steps into the field.

"I repeat," said the weird voice. "Cease, earthlings!"

"Wh-h-ho said that?" the brave but momentarily flustered Howie demanded.

"It is I!" came the answer.

"Whoever it is knows the rudiments of good grammar," Delilah whispered to Howie.

Howie made a mental note to revise Delilah *soon.*

"It's coming from over there," Delilah pointed out, indicating a large tree to their right.

Howie followed Delilah's gaze. "Trees don't talk," he observed.

"That is true," the weird voice responded. "But *I* do!"

Suddenly, a squirrel scampered down the trunk from where it had been hiding among the tree's branches.

"It's just a squirrel," said Howie.

"Yes," said Delilah. "But that is no ordinary squirrel. That is a squirrel . . . FROM ASTEROID 6!!!!!!"

CHAPTER 3:
"THE TERRIBLE AND CREEPY TRANSFORMATION OF DELILAH!"

The squirrel threw back its head and chortled menacingly. In the process, it began choking on a nut it had forgotten was stored in one of its cheeks, but that little episode didn't last long.

"So!" it said, spitting out bits of nut. "You are a *smart* earthling! You know I am from Asteroid 6!"

"Of course," Delilah said. "Anyone who

has ever studied intergalactic biology recognizes a squirrel from Asteroid 6 when she sees one!"

Howie looked at Delilah in amazement.

"Well," said the squirrel, "that is where your so-called intelligence has played a trick on you!"

"What do you mean?" Delilah asked.

"Yeah, what do you mean?" Howie echoed. "My girlfriend's intelligence is not so-called. It's real!"

Delilah sighed and fluttered her long and beautiful eyelashes. "Did you call me your girlfriend?" she asked. "Oh, Howie!"

"Oh, Delilah," Howie said.

"Oh, brother," said the squirrel from Asteroid 6.

Howie and Delilah continued to gaze into each other's eyes.

"I'll wait," the squirrel said.

"Oh, sorry," said the romantic but also level-headed Howie. "You were saying?"

"Why say anything when actions speak louder than words?" said the squirrel. A blue circle of light began to shimmer in the center of his forehead.

Howie and Delilah were riveted to the spot. Not only that, they couldn't move.

The blue light grew brighter and brighter, and then . . . SUDDENLY, IT SHOT OUT OF THE SQUIRREL'S FOREHEAD AND WENT STRAIGHT TO DELILAH'S FOREHEAD! In a flash, the light was gone!

"Delilah!" Howie, the emotionally sensitive yet manly puppy, cried out.

"Help me, Howie!" Delilah's voice cried back.

But her voice wasn't coming from the puppy at Howie's side. It was coming from the squirrel!

HOWIE'S WRITING JOURNAL

Uncle Harold says he thinks what I've written is good, although he pointed out that I called Chapter 2 "The Strange Sound," but never told what the strange sound was. I said I'd fix it, no problem. (Writing is easy.)

Then he said he liked the part where Delilah's voice comes out of the squirrel, but he wondered if my readers would believe that a squirrel could talk in the first place. "Who ever heard of talking squirrels?" he asked.

I said, "Who ever heard of talking dogs?"

"Good point," he said.

So, let's see, I have to come up with a way to let the reader know what the strange sound is, and, oh yeah, I'm definitely going to have to make Delilah not so smart. I mean, where does she come up with all that stuff about the speed of sound and intergalactic biology?!

CHAPTER 4:
"THAT STRANGE SOUND YOU HEARD WAS A FLYING SAUCER!"

"That strange sound you heard was a flying saucer!" said the squirrel. Except its voice was coming out of Delilah's mouth.

Howie looked back and forth between Delilah and the squirrel. Which one was which?

"Are you the squirrel from Asteroid 6?" he asked Delilah.

"Yes," said Delilah—or the puppy formerly known as Delilah. "But I'm not really a squirrel, either. I swapped minds with a squirrel. And now I swapped again with your friend."

"Then who are you really?" Howie asked.

"I told you, he's a squirrel from Asteroid 6!" Delilah shouted out from where she was hanging upside down on the tree trunk.

Howie's head was spinning. He was thinking it would be a good time for a nap, but he didn't want to lose the reader's interest.

"That is where you are wrong, Miss Smarty Pants!" said the squirrel (or whatever he was) from Delilah's mouth. "You may think you know so much with your intergalactic biology, but I am not a squirrel at all. I'm a Mind Swapper from Asteroid 6!"

There was a thundering roar like a herd of buffalo or the anger of the gods on Mount Olympus or what it would sound like if you lived underneath a bowling alley.

Suddenly, there, in the middle of a field of wildflowers on a beautiful summer's day in the peaceful little village of Centerville, where up until this moment life had been normal and calm and people left their houses unlocked and kids played outside until dusk when their mothers called out, "Tommy, Susie, dinner!" and they would come running (if their names were Tommy or Susie)—there, there, before Howie's amazed and befuddled (yet piercing and highly photogenic) eyes, a giant object the shape of a food dish, glowing with a blinding white light, rose up and hovered in the air.

"*That,*" said the Mind Swapper from Asteroid 6, "is the Mother Ship."

"Where's the father ship?" Howie asked. "Stuck in traffic?"

Apparently, the Mind Swapper from Asteroid 6 was not in the mood for a joke. "Silence, earthling!"

Without warning, the Mind Swapper bolted in the direction of the Mother Ship.

The brave and courageous, not to mention daring, Howie had no choice but to follow. It may have been a Mind Swapper, but it was wearing Delilah's body.

"Wait for me!" cried out the equally brave and courageous, although not quite as daring, Delilah, who was wearing the body of a squirrel.

A door opened on the side of the glowing spacecraft.

"Enter!" said an echoey voice that sounded like it was coming from inside an overturned garbage pail. (Howie knew this from the time he'd gotten stuck inside an overturned garbage pail and had had to endure the sound of his own incessant barking bouncing back at him.) (Until it occurred to him to stop barking.) (And knock over the garbage pail.) (And go home.)

Steps lowered to the ground. The Mind Swapper ran up the steps. Howie gasped as he watched Delilah—or her body—disappear from sight.

"Enter!!" the overturned-garbage-pail voice commanded.

31

"Don't!!" Delilah (the squirrel) called out.

Howie put one paw on the first step. He felt himself being pulled against his will toward the inside of the flying food dish. He *had* to save Delilah!

But who was Delilah? Was she the beautiful puppy harboring the evil mind of the creature from Asteroid 6? Or was she the keenly intelligent brain trapped in the body of a tree-climbing rodent? And if Howie went aboard the spacecraft, what would protect him from having his own mind swapped? But if he didn't go inside the spacecraft, how would Delilah's body and mind get back together? But if he did go aboard, would he be taken to Asteroid 6 and never see his family again? But if he didn't go aboard, would he regret it for all the days of his life? (And if he doesn't stop asking all these questions, will we ever get to the next chapter?)

Suddenly, the spacecraft began to shake.

"Too late!!" cried the voice from inside.

Howie tumbled backward onto the ground as the steps were sucked back into the Mother Ship and, with a great roar, the spacecraft lifted up, up, up, and then . . . *vanished* before his eyes!

The air was full of silence. And pollen.

Howie sneezed. "Delilah . . ." he called out weakly.

"Right here," said a voice behind him.

Howie turned and saw that Delilah (the squirrel) was nibbling on something she held in her tiny paws.

"These acorns aren't half bad," she told him. "Care to try one?"

HOWIE'S WRITING JOURNAL

Oh, great. Now Delilah's not speaking to me again.

"A squirrel?" she said. "You've turned me into a <u>squirrel</u>? And before that, you made me as stupid as you did in the first book, and then you made me so smart I sounded like I had a computer for a brain! You know what I think your problem is, Howie? I think your problem is that you don't know how to write girl characters!"

I told her that was not true!! I said, "Look at Chapter 1–'Delilah tossed her blonde ears and cocked her head to one side.' If that isn't good writing about girl characters, what is?!"

I don't remember exactly what the next thing she said was, but the next thing I said was, "Ouch."

Writing is dangerous.

CHAPTER 5:
"DELILAH, THE
INTELLIGENT SQUIRREL"

"Follow me," Howie, a natural-born leader, told Delilah.

Delilah scampered along at his side. "Where are we going?" she asked. She then reminded him that even though she looked like a squirrel, she was still smart and deserving of his respect.

"I know that," said Howie, "although you

are not as smart as you were in Chapters 2 and 3, when you sounded like you had a computer for a brain."

"And no one is saying squirrels aren't intelligent," Delilah added, wanting to be sure that Howie didn't get in trouble with some organization like the Friends of Squirrels when his book was published.

"That is very true," Howie said, grateful that Delilah was thinking of him. "Now, to answer your question: Where we are going is to Centerville College, where Mr. Monroe teaches. Of course, Mr. Monroe teaches *English,* which doesn't exactly help us, but there must be a scientist in the Astrofizziology department who can help us figure out what's going on and how to get you—er, your body—back from outer space."

"Cool," said Delilah, batting her squirrelly eyelashes at Howie. These were not as beautiful as her old eyelashes, but Howie was flattered nonetheless. Although it was weird to have a squirrel batting her eyelashes at him.

Once they got to Centerville College, Howie said, "You'd better leave this to me, Delilah. Not because you're not smart or anything . . ."

"Of course not," Delilah said.

"It's just that, being one of his pets and all, Mr. Monroe knows me. Somehow I have to communicate to him that I need his help. Anyway, if you're with me, he might wonder what I'm doing hanging around with a squirrel. Usually, I'm chasing them."

"I understand, Howie," Delilah replied calmly. "I'll wait out here in this beautiful park, where I can scamper and frolic and beg for popcorn."

"Okay," Howie said sadly, for he could not help but think that for the rest of her life, Delilah might be destined to scamper and frolic and beg for popcorn. She might never again know the joys of playing Rip-the-Rag or chewing on old sneakers or sniffing hydrants! And they might never marry! And if they *did* marry, what would their children look like? He *had* to rescue her body and reunite it with her mind!

But on his way to Mr. Monroe's office, he saw terrible things that made him think Delilah was not the only one affected by the recent visit of the . . . **Mind Swappers from Asteroid 6!**

Howie's Writing Journal

Uncle Harold said, "Howie, changing the font on your computer doesn't count as writing!"

I said, "What do you mean, Uncle Harold?"

He said, "You don't build suspense just by putting the words 'Mind Swappers from Asteroid 6' in some fancy font."

I said, "But I thought it looked cool. See, it's like a logo kind of thing, you know, like you identify it with the book. So when the movie comes out and all the toys and stuff, they'll use the same font, and then consumers will know what they're getting. That's called 'brand-name recognition.' Toby did a report on it for school. It's very important to know your market, Uncle Harold."

Uncle Harold groaned and rolled his eyes. I asked him if he felt okay. He mumbled something about what the world was coming to, and went off to take a nap.

Too bad. I wanted to ask him if I should be putting a trademark sign over the title. You know, like this:

Invasion of the Mind Swappers

from Asteroid 6!™

He probably would have said no. I used to think Uncle Harold was totally awesome, but I'm beginning to think he's a little old-fashioned. I mean, doesn't he know that cool fonts have <u>everything</u> to do with writing?!

CHAPTER 6:
"THE HORRIBLE
FATE OF CENTERVILLE"

As he made his way across the campus of Centerville College, Howie noticed that the students were acting very strangely.

"Soon we will command the . . . oops, an earthling," he heard one girl say as she walked past him. Actually, he had to look up to make sure it was a girl, because she had this weird metallic voice.

She was walking with a boy whose blank eyes were staring straight ahead. *Wow*, Howie thought, *he must have had a hard day at school.*

But then he heard the boy say in this flat voice that sounded like it had been run over by a steamroller, "Yes, soon our mission here will be complete."

Howie, being the perceptive and insightful wirehaired dachshund puppy that he was, sensed that something wasn't quite right. Why were these students talking so strangely? Perhaps they were drama students practicing lines from a play. But there was something about their use of the word "earthling." Where had Howie heard it before?

Just then, Howie heard his name being called. It sounded like this:

"Howie! Howie!"

It was Toby, the Monroes' youngest son! (And smartest.) (And neatest.)

(And nicest.)

(Not that Howie didn't like Pete, the Monroes' other son.)

What was Toby doing here at Centerville College?

"Oh, Howie," Toby called out as he threw his arms around his popular and beloved pet. "Am I ever glad to see you, boy! *You'll* know what to do!"

"Do?" Howie said, although it came out: "Woof?"

"Something terrible's happened to Dad! Mom dropped me off at his office about twenty minutes ago so I could use his copy machine and he . . . he . . ." Toby started to sniffle.

"I'm sorry, boy," he said. "I don't want to cry, but Dad . . . he just isn't acting like himself. He keeps spinning around in his chair and saying something like, 'Must get chairs like this for Asteroid 6.' And his voice is all flat, like it's been run over by a steamroller. What is it, Howie? Is it something he ate? Is he sick? Is he going crazy?"

"No," Howie said, "it's none of those things. It's worse. Mr. Monroe is an innocent victim of the **Invasion of the Mind Swappers from Asteroid 6!**™ His mind has been swapped with an evil alien's, and I believe the students I heard earlier were also mind-swapping victims! Perhaps all of Centerville has been

drained of its brains, Toby. Perhaps you and I are the only ones left!"

Although it came out: "Woof!"

"We've got to save Dad!" Toby cried. "But how, how? You're smart, Howie. You lead the way and I'll follow!"

Howie was smart, it was true, but he didn't know where to go, what to do. He had hoped Mr. Monroe might know somebody in the Astrofizziology department, but Mr. Monroe's mind wasn't available since it was on the Mother Ship on its way to Asteroid 6!

Just then, the sky turned white!!!!

HOWIE'S WRITING JOURNAL

Writing is so cool! I didn't know what to have Howie do next, so I turned the sky white! Of course, now I have to figure out why the sky turned white, but that'll be easier than having to figure out what Howie should do next.

CHAPTER 7: "THE DAY THE SKY TURNED WHITE"

"There! It's up there!" Howie heard someone shout.

He looked up but couldn't see a thing because the sky had turned white. A blinding white. Like the inside of the sun. Or the T-shirts in TV commercials for laundry detergent. Or some movie star's teeth.

Suddenly, he heard his name being called.

It sounded like this: "Howie! Howie!"

Except it was kind of quiet, as if someone small was calling it. More like, "Howie! Howie!" A squirrel, maybe.

"There you are!" Delilah cried. "I've been looking for you everywhere!"

"What is it, Howie?" Toby asked. "What's made the sky turn white?" Noticing the squirrel, he asked, "And who's your friend?"

"It's Delilah," Howie explained. "But you can't recognize her because her mind is trapped in a squirrel's body."

Although it came out . . . oh, you know how it came out.

Just then, there was a distant roar of thunder.

"That sound," said Howie. "Could it be . . . ?"

"The Mother Ship!" Delilah said. "Judging

from the decibel level and considering that the air quality today is at an all-time—"

"Stop that!" Howie snapped. "You've been revised. Did you forget?"

"Oh, sorry," said Delilah. Then she repeated: "The Mother Ship!"

Delilah was right. Even Howie had to admit it. Although he didn't like to.

"You're right!" he said.

The white light began to fade, and there in the sky was the giant spacecraft Howie and Delilah had seen earlier.

"Look!" Delilah cried. "There I am! I've got my head hanging out the window! Do you see how my ears are flapping in the wind? I always did like going for rides and hanging my head out the window." A tear fell from her eye.

"I'll get your body back," the heroic dachshund told Delilah's mind. "If those **Mind Swappers from Asteroid 6!**™ think they can mess with Howie Monroe, they've got another think coming!"

"Oh, Howie," Delilah sighed, batting her eyelashes and offering him an acorn she'd been stashing in her left cheek.

Howie looked at the woman he loved and heaved a heavy and heroic sigh.

If I fail at my mission, he thought, *I'll be spending the rest of my life eating acorns.*

It was a chilling thought.

HOWIE'S WRITING JOURNAL

Oh, fine. Delilah reminded me I was supposed to make <u>her</u> the heroic one in this book. How am I supposed to do that? She's a <u>squirrel</u>!

CHAPTER 8:
"DELILAH TO THE RESCUE"

There in the sky was the giant spacecraft Howie and Delilah had seen earlier.

"Look!" Delilah cried. "There I am! I've got my head hanging out the window! Do you see how my ears are flapping in the wind? I always did like going for rides and hanging my head out the window." A tear fell from her eye.

"I'll get my body back," the heroic squirrel

said. "If those **Mind Swappers from Asteroid 6!**™ think they can mess with Delilah, they've got another think coming!"

"Oh, Delilah," Howie sighed, batting his eyelashes and accepting the acorn she offered him. "You are so heroic."

"It's true," Delilah agreed. "All I have to figure out now is what to do. Can you help?"

"Sure thing," said Howie.

Just then, the spacecraft landed.

A roar rose up from the crowd: "All hail the conquering **Mind Swappers from Asteroid 6!**™"

Howie looked around in alarm. On all sides of him stood the citizens of Centerville, their eyes as empty as a can of Mighty-Dog after it's been scraped clean and Mrs. Monroe can't get one more bit of food out of it even if you whimper and wish with all your heart she could. They stood in a wide circle around the Mother Ship—the children and parents and professors and students and dogs and cats and barbers and dentists and race-car drivers and yoga instructors and piano tuners and . . . well, you get the picture . . . *everybody* in Centerville was standing there staring vacantly and murmuring, "Hail, hail, hail."

"Look," Toby cried. "There's Dad. And Mom too. And Pete's there with Harold and Chester."

Toby started to run toward his family, but Howie, the wise and intelligent, not to mention smart, dachshund puppy, caught the cuff of Toby's pants in his teeth. He couldn't speak

at that moment, having a mouth full of pants and all, but if he could, he would have said, "It's no use! Your family's minds have been swapped with the minds of the creatures from Asteroid 6! If you get too close to them, what you behold will only break your heart!"

Toby seemed to understand. "Look at them," he said. "It's as if their minds have been swapped with the minds of the creatures in that spaceship. If I get too close to them, what I behold will only break my heart."

As Toby crumpled to the ground, Howie released his pants leg. He would taste denim for the rest of the afternoon.

Howie wanted to assure Toby that it would be all right, that his family would be the way they always were. But how could that be? What could he do? He was only one small dachshund in a world gone mad, one tiny voice in a sea of voices, one pebble in a field of boulders, one itsy-bitsy minnow in a school of sharks!

Still, he had to do something. The future of the world rested on his small, but surprisingly strong and able, shoulders.

Then he remembered that it was Delilah's turn to be the hero. *What a relief,* he thought. *I don't have to figure this out, after all.*

CHAPTER 8:
"DELILAH TO THE RESCUE"

"Well?" said Delilah.

"Well what?" Howie retorted cleverly.

"I thought you were going to help me," Delilah said.

"I can't," Howie told her. "If I think of what to do, then *I'll* be the hero. And it's your turn, remember?"

Delilah sighed. "I remember," she said.

Howie and Delilah looked at each other for a long time.

Howie was getting hungry.

Even an acorn sounded good.

The story came to a standstill.

HOWIE'S WRITING JOURNAL

I HAVE WRITER'S BLOCK!!!!!!!!!!!!!!!!!!

I went to Uncle Harold.

I said, "Uncle Harold, what do you do when you have writer's block?"

He said, "I take a nap."

I tried that, but when I woke up I still had writer's block.

(I think Uncle Harold's solution to everything is to take a nap.) (Or eat.)

So I asked Pop for some advice. "Pop" is what I call the cat who lives with us. His real name is Chester, and he is very, very smart. I knew he would have good advice for me.

"Are you still writing those inane stories?" he said. "Give up. You're a dog, for heaven's sake. Go bury a bone and get over your delusions."

Sometimes Pop uses words I don't understand. Like "inane" and "delusions."

And "give up."

What am I going to do? I'm really stuck!

If I can't write this story, my first one

won't get published. Then I'll never be famous and have my picture on the cover of <u>Canine</u> <u>Quarterly</u>.

I think I'll take another nap.

Or eat.

HOWIE'S WRITING JOURNAL

I've got it!

The answer!

I'll ask Delilah (the real one) what she would do!

HOWIE'S WRITING JOURNAL

Delilah really <u>is</u> smart. She figured the whole thing out for me. First, she said, something <u>really</u> <u>threatening</u> has to happen. And then all I have to do is ask myself what a really smart dog (like her), who happens to be trapped in the body of a squirrel, would do.

It's like Uncle Harold always says: "Just ask enough questions and you'll come up with a story."

CHAPTER 8:
"DELILAH TO THE RESCUE!"

Suddenly, the door of the spacecraft opened! The steps Howie and Delilah had seen earlier magically lowered. The crowd held its breath. It sounded like this:

"   "

It kept holding its breath . . .

"   "

. . . until, as if it were one, it gasped! A

green space creature with a head the shape of an egg emerged from the Mother Ship and raised one of its three hands in a salute. "Greep tabbo-tabbo!" it said in its flat metallic voice.

"Greep tabbo-tabbo!" said the citizens of Centerville. Even the dogs and cats. Even Harold and Chester.

"I don't understand," Howie said. "What's happening?"

"Isn't it obvious?" said Delilah. "That's the leader of the **Mind Swappers from Asteroid 6!**™ It's greeting the others, who are responding in the tongue of their home asteroid because, although these may look like familiar faces, everyone around us is really a **Mind Swapper from Asteroid 6!**™"

"I feel so . . . so alone," Howie whimpered.

"So . . . so vulnerable. You have to do something, Delilah!"

"But what can I do? I am only one small squirrel in a world gone mad, one tiny voice in a sea of voices, one pebble in a field of boulders, one itsy-bitsy minnow in a school of sharks!"

Just then, another creature stepped out onto the platform at the top of the stairs. And then another and another, until the platform was filled with green, three-armed creatures.

And there in the middle of them all was the dog formerly known as Delilah!

"It's me!" Delilah cried. "I *must* be reunited with my body! But wait! If I want to be reunited so badly, what about the squirrel? Surely the squirrel—"

"How do you know the squirrel's name is Shirley?" Howie asked, hoping to inject some much-needed humor into the narrative.

Delilah gave him a dirty look. "Surely . . . the . . . squirrel . . . must want to return to its body as well. But the squirrel's mind is not in *my* body; it's in the body of one of these creatures. If I can just find the right creature, I may be able to set in motion a chain reaction that's calculated at the rate of—"

She was cut off by the words of the leader of the Mind Swappers.

"Sling mahu wangee olgie deep!" he said, holding aloft a flag with a picture of an asteroid on it.

"They're about to take over Planet Earth!" Howie, the keenly insightful dachshund, pointed out. "Hurry, Delilah, you've got to act *now!*"

Delilah sprang into action.

Scampering up the stairs, she rushed through the legs of the space creatures, who responded by saying things like, "Oogoo," and "Mageeha," and "Watch where you're going!"

What was she up to? Howie wondered. He had a pretty good idea, but he kept it to himself so that Delilah could be the hero of the story.

The crowd below watched intently as this seemingly ordinary squirrel ran from space creature to space creature, holding something up in its paw. What was it? Howie strained to see.

Then he made it out. Yes, he thought so: It was an acorn!

Suddenly, one of the aliens bent down and grabbed the acorn from Delilah's paw. "Eek, eek!" it squeaked as it shoved the acorn into its greedy mouth.

But this was not space-talk. This was squirrel-talk! Delilah had found the creature that held the squirrel's brain.

Now that she had found him, she skittered up his leg until she reached his shoulders. There, she gazed intently into his eyes. (All four of them.)

A blue light began to glow in the middle of the space creature's forehead. It glowed deeper and deeper in color until all at once it shot out in an arc to Delilah's forehead. No sooner had it reached the squirrel than it faded away.

The squirrel, looking bewildered, scrambled

down the creature's body, off the platform, and down the stairs, until it reached the safety of a tree. Up it went into the high branches.

"Delilah!" Howie called out. "Where are you going?"

"I'm not going anywhere," the space creature who had just eaten the acorn replied. "I'm right here!"

CHAPTER 9:
"DROOL FOR YOUR LIFE!"

Delilah (the space creature) scooped Delilah (the dog, but with the space creature's mind) up in her arms and held her out in front of her. "Look at me!" she commanded.

The dog turned its head this way and that so rapidly Howie was afraid it might get whiplash.

"Look into my eyes!" Delilah commanded again.

"No, no!" the dog replied.

"If you don't, I will see that you live the rest of your days in the body of this dog. You will have to eat from a bowl on the floor forever, and little girls will put bows in your hair and call you their baby!"

The dog stopped its thrashing at once.

Staring into the eyes of the space creature, it made a blue circle appear in the middle of its forehead. A ray of light shot from one forehead to the other.

Suddenly, the Mind Swapper dropped the dog to the ground. She scampered down the steps and ran toward Howie.

"I'm free, I'm free!" Delilah yipped. "But now I must save the others."

"But how?" Howie asked, knowing perfectly

well he could figure it out if *he* were the hero of the story.

"It's simple, really," Delilah said. "You see, once the Mind Swapper realized that—"

"Don't you mean the **Mind Swapper from Asteroid 6!**™?" Howie asked.

"Right," said Delilah. "Well, anyway, once it realized that staying inside my body meant living like a dog, it wanted *out!* All we have to do is convince the other Mind Swappers—uh, **Mind Swappers from Asteroid 6!**™—that they wouldn't want to be stuck inside the bodies of earthlings, either, and they'll swap their minds back, too!"

"Easier said than done," the philosophical Howie replied.

"Yes, but where there's a will, there's a way,"

the equally philosophical Delilah replied back.

Just then, Toby ran over to the two dogs. "Howie! Delilah!" he shouted. "What's going on? Delilah, why were you in that flying saucer?"

"No time to explain," Delilah yipped as she leaped up at Toby and began licking his face.

"What are you doing, you silly mutt?" Toby cried. "Stop, stop!"

As Toby tried to bat Delilah away, Delilah called over her shoulder to Howie, "Run over to somebody and start slobbering on them!"

"What?"

"Do what I'm telling you!" Delilah ordered. "Drool, drool for your life!"

Howie, sensing the brilliance behind Delilah's plan, worked up some saliva and chose one of the college students as his victim.

"Iggo ucko pooey!" the college student said in Asteroid Sixian.

Roughly translated, she was saying, "This is disgusting, and if you think I'm going to stick around on this planet and be covered in slime by some hyperactive creature who, may I point out, also *sheds,* you've got another think coming!"

A circle of blue light appeared in the middle of her forehead. Howie stopped his slobbering long enough to watch as the arc of light went out from her forehead and reached the forehead of one of the Mind Swappers on the deck of the Mother Ship.

Suddenly, the girl's eyes snapped shut, then open, and she said, "Oh, thank goodness, I'm

me at last! I'm free at last! And all because of one very smart dog and one slobbery one!"

Howie tried not to be insulted.

The next thing he knew, each and every forehead in the crowd began to glow with a blue light. Pretty soon, all the **Mind Swappers from Asteroid 6!**™ were back on the Mother Ship and all the citizens of Centerville were back to normal.

And all because of Delilah!

(And Howie too, but mostly because of Delilah.)

Just before the Mother Ship took off to return to whence from which it came, the leader of the **Invasion of the Mind Swappers from Asteroid 6!**™ stepped forward and spoke.

(No one knew how it was that these creatures sometimes knew English. It is one of the great mysteries of the universe.)

"We leave in peace!" the Mind Swapper proclaimed. "Okay, I admit we didn't come in peace, but we're leaving in peace, so that's what counts, right? We intended to take over Planet Earth because we didn't have enough room on our asteroid. It's pretty small, and the way our population keeps growing, the rents are killing us. But on Asteroid 6, we do not have to endure the saliva of lowly creatures. This would be too much for us to take. It is gross and unsanitary and, on top of that, it tickles.

"We apologize for any inconvenience our stay here may have caused you. When I snap my fingers, you will forget this ever happened. Have a nice day."

With that, the Mother Ship vanished into thin air, and all the citizens of Centerville awoke as if from a dream.

"Want to play Rip-the-Rag?" Delilah asked Howie.

"Great," Howie replied. "Then can we play Knock-Each-Other-Down?"

They played games all afternoon and never remembered a thing that had happened that terrible day.

(Although they couldn't help but feel it had something to do with Delilah's sudden and enduring fondness for acorns.)

THE END

HOWIE'S WRITING JOURNAL

Uncle Harold said my story is ready to be sent to his editor! I'm going to be famous!

I wonder if it will change me. Will I have to wear sunglasses all the time? I don't think I'd like that. I bump into things too much as it is. But maybe I can get a Jacuzzi!

I asked Uncle Harold about it.

He said, "I've written many books and I

don't wear sunglasses and I don't have a Jacuzzi."

I found this discouraging. "Then why write?" I asked.

"Keep writing," he advised me. "You'll find out."

I think Uncle Harold has been listening to too many of Mr. Monroe's Zen meditation tapes. What kind of answer is that?

Maybe I'll just have to keep writing. Besides, Delilah says I still have a ways to go in knowing how to write girl characters. So I'd better get started on my next book.

But first I'm going to take a nap. Maybe I'll dream about being famous.

And having a Jacuzzi.